D0001514

THE STORY OF IRON MAN

Adapted by Thomas Macri
Illustrated by Craig Rousseau *and* Hi-Fi Design
Based on the Marvel comic book series Iron Man

ABD
Spotlight

WWW.ABDOPUBLISHING.COM

Reinforced library bound edition published in 2015 by Spotlight, a division of ABDO
PO Box 398166, Minneapolis, Minnesota 55439. Spotlight produces high-quality
reinforced library bound editions for schools and libraries. Published by Marvel Press,
an imprint of Disney Book Group.

Printed in the United States of America, North Mankato, Minnesota.
052014
072014

marvelkids.com

TM & © 2013 Marvel & Subs.

THIS BOOK CONTAINS
RECYCLED MATERIALS

LIBRARY OF CONGRESS CATALOGING-IN-PUBLICATION DATA

This title was previously cataloged with the following information:

Macri, Thomas.
 The story of Ironman / adapted by Thomas Macri ; illustrated by Craig Rousseau and
Hi-Fi Design.
  p. cm. -- (World of reading. Level 2)
Summary: Learn how Tony Stark became the super hero known as Iron Man.
1. Iron Man (Fictitious character)--Juvenile fiction. 2. Superheroes--Juvenile fiction. I.
Rousseau, Craig, ill. II. Hi-Fi Colour Design, ill. III. Title. IV. Series.
PZ7.M24731Ss 2012
[E]--dc23

2012286172

978-1-61479-259-8 (Reinforced Library Bound Edition)

Spotlight

A Division of ABDO
www.abdopublishing.com

Tony Stark was good at making things. He met with the Army. They wanted him to help them.

Tony worked in an Army lab. Something exploded! An enemy had attacked.

They wanted Tony to make weapons.
They took him away.

They took him to a cell. He met
another prisoner. His name was
Yinsen.

Yinsen made things, too.

He put a hand on Tony's shoulder.

Tony's heart was hurt.

Yinsen built something to help. It would keep Tony's heart beating. He would always have to wear it. It would keep him alive.

They also made a suit of armor.
Tony would wear it. It would help
them escape.

Now Tony could break anything.
He smashed through a brick wall.

He fought the whole enemy army.

He won easily.

The enemy was scared.
They ran away.

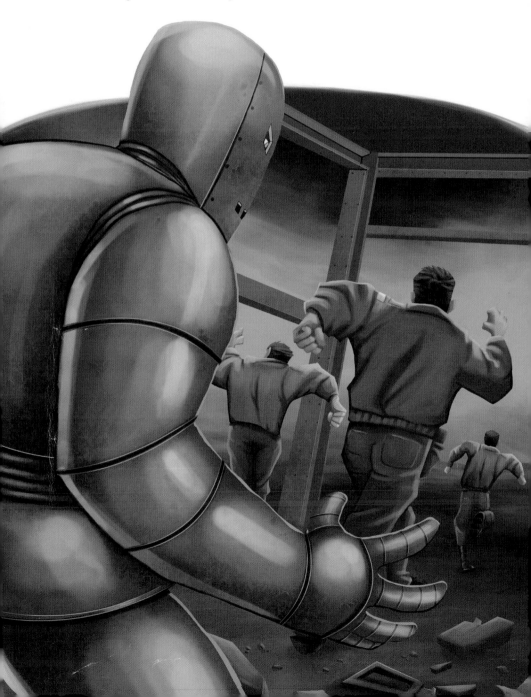

Tony escaped. He used his suit
to fly home.

Tony wanted to help others. On TV
he saw a crime happening.

He flew over to help.

Everyone was scared.
The people he was there to save
were scared, too.
His armor was too scary.

Tony painted his armor. Now people
would not be scared of him.

His armor was still not perfect.
He still needed to fix it up.

Tony made his suit light.
He painted it red and gold.

He made a powerful energy force.
He shot it from his hands.

He shot it from his boots. The suit could now fly fast.

He had to think of a Super Hero name.
He chose Iron Man.

Iron Man fought Super Villains.

Sometimes he fought two!

He could attack from behind.

He could pick up bad guys.

Tony kept on fixing up the armor. He used special tools. He put on goggles. He worked all the time.

Tony did not always wear a suit
of armor.
Sometimes he wore a suit and tie.

He always kept a suitcase near.
It had his armor inside.

He never knew when the world would
need Iron Man!